THE FARMINGTON COMMUNITY LIBRARY
FARMINGTON HILLS BR
32737 WEST TWELVE MIL
FARMINGTON HILLS, MI 48334-3302
(248) 553-0300

W9-DET-115

FARMINGTON COMMUNITY LIBRARY

3 0036 01330 0031

OCT 2 3 2019

Clara Vulliamy

THE VACATION MYSTERY

Dotty
DETECTIVE

HarperCollins *Children's Books*

First published in Great Britain by HarperCollins
Children's Books in 2018
First published in the United States of America in this edition by
HarperCollins *Children's Books* 2019
HarperCollins *Children's Books* is a division of HarperCollins*Publishers* Ltd,
1 London Bridge Street, London, SE1 9GF

The HarperCollins website address is: www.harpercollins.co.uk

1

Text and illustrations copyright © Clara Vulliamy 2018
All rights reserved.

ISBN 978-0-00-830091-3

Clara Vulliamy asserts the moral right to be identified as the
author and illustrator of the work.

Printed and bound by CPI Group (UK) Ltd, Croydon, CR0 4YY

Conditions of Sale
This book is sold subject to the condition that it shall not, by way of trade
or otherwise, be lent, re-sold, hired out or otherwise circulated without the
publisher's prior consent in any form, binding or cover other than that
in which it is published and without a similar condition including this
condition being imposed on the subsequent purchaser.

Find out more about HarperCollins and the environment at
www.harpercollins.co.uk/green

3 0036 01330 0031

For Harriet, with much love

Read the whole series:

This book belongs to . . .

DOT

and McClusky

FRIDAY

This is me, Dorothy Constance Mae Louise, but all of my friends just call me ⭰Dot!⭰

And here is my family: Mom, my twin brother and sister, Alf and Maisy, and my dog, McClusky.

Rushing to school in an absolute **BLUR** today, *extremely* excited, because it's the last day of term and then **SUMMER VACATION BEGINS!**

In class, our teacher, Mr. Dickens, says, "Today we will play *games* instead of having lessons!"

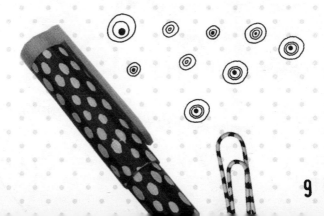

We all whoop and shout, "Yay!
Hooray! Wowzers!" until Frankie gets
carried away with *his* "Wowzers!" and
sends a pile of books flying.

We play board games and bingo.
Amy crosses her numbers off first
and wins a pair of
**googly-eye
glasses!**

And then we play **Who Am I?**

We get into pairs and each person has a name they can't see written on a **post-it note** stuck to their forehead.

Mr. Dickens

You ask your partner questions about who you are, but they can only answer "YES" or "NO".

Me and my best friend Beans are in a pair and we are REALLY QUICK to guess who we are!

This is because we are not *just* best friends, OH NO . . .

We are also TOP super-sleuthing secret agents, the Join the Dots Detectives!

JOIN THE DOTS DETECTIVES

Which makes us very good at asking the right questions and super-speedy at finding out the **vital facts.**

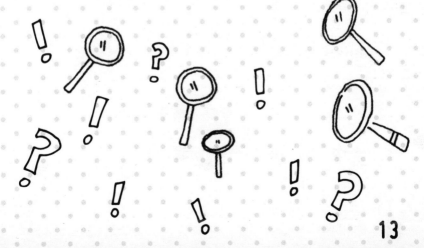

Heading to the school gate at dismissal, everyone is talking about what they will be doing on their summer vacation.

The **EXTRA-FANTASTIC** thing about this summer is that me (and the twins and Mom and McClusky) and Beans (and his dad) are going on vacation to the same place TOMORROW!

We are going to

Sunny Glades Campsite

by the seaside.

I CAN'T WAIT!!

15

"Are you bringing your detective kit, Beans?" I ask.

"I'm bringing a FEW things, like my flashlights and my code book," says Beans. "You just never know. . . ."

eye patch

DUSTING for Footprints

? ? ? ? ?
THOUSANDS
OF AMAZING
SECRET CODES
? ? ? ? ? ?

FALSE
MOUSTACHES

I have my packing list in my pocket.
I add some essential stationery for
drawing maps, making suspect lists,
and writing down clues, just in case.

sun hat

bathing suit

lobster
cover-up

snorkle

flip-flops

notebook

TOP
SECRET

pens

We walk home via the main street for some last-minute vacation shopping.

Mom buys sunscreen that—

MMMMMm! — smells like BUBBLEGUM!

The twins choose some tiny paper flags for their **sandcastles** . . .

and I choose some summer vacation *stickers*.

19

At home, me and McClusky try on LOTS of *different* sunglasses. We absolutely *cannot* decide which suit us best, so we pack them all.

SQUEEEEEEEZE! There's JUST room in my suitcase for my **extra-big** new puzzle book I've been saving specially …

and we are all packed and ready for the morning!

Saturday

We get up really early. The camper trailer is hitched up ...

The car is PACKED FULL TO BURSTING...

and we're off!

McClusky goes **crazy** with joy on car journeys. I give him a Calming Chew Doggy Treat every now and then and he settles down, but still **wiggles** in his sleep as if he's already imagining **running** across the beach!

And here we are—arriving at
Sunny Glades Campsite!
We drive in and park our camper. On
one side are woods, and on the other
an **enormous** tent with lots of
little children rushing in and out.

Inside, our camper is like a little
house—everything the same but
small! A little fridge, a little oven . . .

The floor is **red**-and-white check, and there are strawberry-patterned curtains *all* the way around, with cushions to match.

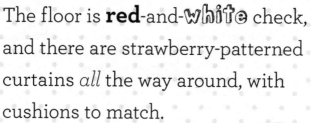

We unpack our things. The seats fold out into beds and we arrange our sleeping bags in a row.

Then I **hurry** over to find Beans. His dad is **struggling** to get their tent up, so Mom figures it out while he puts the kettle on their camping stove and searches for teabags and *cookies.*

It's *even smaller* inside their tent, with room for just two airbeds. Me and Beans take it in turns to **blow** them up with the **foot pump**. It's HARD WORK!

"The simple life for us, back to nature!" says Beans's dad, nibbling a cookie, while Mom hammers in a tent peg.

PLAYGROUND
***** *
fun for all ages!

When we have finished unpacking,
me, Beans, and the twins explore
the campsite. We see **mini golf**
and a **fantastic**
playground. "And
look, Beans!"
I say. **"Bicycles
to rent!** I would
LOVE to do
some cycling."

There's a big farmhouse where the campsite owners live, and a campsite café called the Nook. It's a camper too, but a tiny one with a stripy sunshade and **sparkly** bunting. There are little tables arranged around it, with a vase of *fresh flowers* on each one.

A teenager waves at us through the hatch. She looks **SO COOL**. I have never seen anybody with *turquoise* hair before! The twins can't stop staring.

"Hi, guys!" she says to us with a **huge** smile. "I'm Poppy. Welcome to the Nook! Come and have a look around."

The Nook may be small, but it has a

LOT

of **interesting** things.

Knickknacks are laid out for sale on a table beside the camper—all kinds of *ornaments* and cups and saucers that don't match. Beans is fascinated by the **fossil collection**.

Mom has given me some money to buy us all a **treat**. "What would you like?" I ask the twins. Alf chooses a pink cupcake and Maisy chooses a *yellow* one. After much discussion, me and Beans go for the warm mini doughnuts.

"I *love* doughnuts!" I tell Poppy. "And so does my dog, McClusky!" I put a little piece in my pocket to give to him later.

"Doughnuts are *my life*," says Poppy. "I want to be a chef one day— baking will be my *speciality!*"

Me and Beans agree that these are the **BEST** doughnuts we've ever tasted.

"*Good!*" says Poppy. "I hope you come and hang out at the Nook *lots!*"

Poppy explains that her mom and dad own the campsite and she is in charge of the café. We can tell she works **really hard**—serving guests, bringing drinks and clearing tables.

"It's **CRAZY** here, especially in the summer. I'll soon need a vacation myself," she laughs.

"Busy Poppy!" says Alf.

"Busy bee!" says Maisy.

Poppy is bringing out tea for two
ladies, served in a teapot shaped like
a **lighthouse**. "This is my **lucky teapot!**"
she tells them.

"How beautiful, and *so* unusual!" says the lady in a *pink* sunhat.

"Ooh, *yes!*" says her friend with a *yellow* headscarf. "I wish *we* owned one just like it—we collect teapots, you know!"

The Nook is packed with guests. There's a **grumpy**-looking man at the table next to ours. He orders lots of *different* things to eat, but I notice he only takes **one** bite of each.

Weird!

I wonder who he is?

After we finish our **treats**, we wave goodbye to Poppy and explore a bit more.

Over in the animal enclosure, we meet Fred, a local boy who helps look after the animals. He shows us two donkeys, adopted from a rescue sanctuary, called *Please* and Thankyou ...

* * * *

and some chickens ...

and a tortoise called **Speedy**.

"He's **quicker** than you'd think," says Fred, "and **impossible** to spot when he heads off into the undergrowth— so we tie a **BALLOON** around him. That way, we always know where he is!"

Back in the camper, we find our pajamas and toothbrushes, settle in, and draw the curtains, making everything **cozy** for the evening.

Now I'm **snuggled** down in my sleeping bag at bedtime. McClusky is snoring away in his basket, wedged in between me and the twins. I can still see some **sugar sprinkled** on his nose from the piece of doughnut I saved for him.

I
LOVE
Sunny Glades!

This vacation is going to be

FANTASTIC!

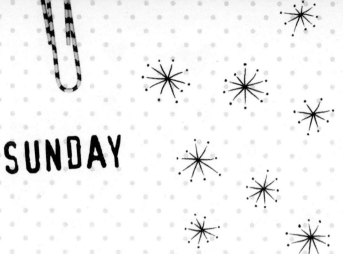

SUNDAY

When I wake up, the twins are still asleep, so I get up quietly and find Mom outside having a cup of tea. It feels really nice to be **up and outdoors** very early.

chirp!

chirp!

All we can hear are the birds

singing

and the leaves in the

trees.

Now McClusky **wakes up**, which means that soon everybody else for **miles** is **awake** too!

WOOF! WOOF!

The little children from the enormous tent next door are running around, shouting and shrieking.

An old couple in the camper across from us peer **grumpily** out of their open window. The woman is arranging some *flowers* on the windowsill. "So much for peace and quiet," the man grumbles, pulling the window shut.

We go over for breakfast at the Nook because Mom hasn't had time to go to the campsite shop yet for groceries.

The twins insist on wearing their
big coats even though it's a warm,
sunny day. They are whispering to each
other in their secret *twinny* language
too. They are **SO STRANGE**
sometimes!

Beans and his dad are already here,
tucking into **cream cheese bagels**.

We order our breakfast:
fresh croissants and

orange juice.

That grumpy man is here again, standing a little way off and looking over at the Nook.

"Who is that man?" we ask Poppy.

"Oh, that's Mr. Blunt," she tells us. "He has just opened a café himself, right down by the sea, called **BLUNT'S BEACH CAFÉ**."

A customer waves to Poppy and she rushes off again.

"Well, *we* won't be going to Blunt's," I whisper to Beans. The Nook is already our favorite café in the whole world!

Beans's dad wanders off with his binoculars to look at birds. Mom is concentrating on her shopping list while the twins finish their breakfast, so me and Beans go over to the playground to try out the tire swing and the **wobbly** plank.

By the time we head back past the Nook, Mom and the twins have left.

We see Poppy on her hands and knees, looking under the tables.

OH NO—she looks very worried.

"My **lighthouse** teapot has VANISHED!" she says. "AND one of my vases of flowers! I can't see them *anywhere*! They are very special to me. Where can they be?"

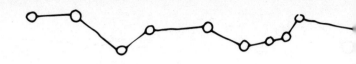

What a calamity!
POOR POPPY!

I look at Beans and he looks at me.
**WE ARE BOTH THINKING
EXACTLY THE SAME THING.**

"There are two people who have
ALL the detectively skills to find the
missing teapot and vase—" I start to
say, and Beans finishes my sentence.

"US!!"

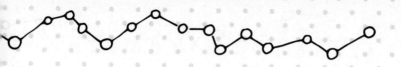

It's the **Sunny Glades** Mystery and the Join the Dots Detectives are ON THE CASE!!

ON THE CASE

Right away we find a quiet place for a secret Join the Dots meeting.

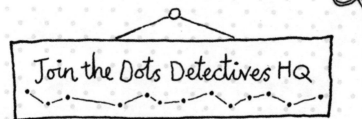

Join the Dots Detectives HQ

"Somebody must have **stolen** the teapot and vase of *flowers*!" I say.

"Yes!" says Beans. "But *who*?"

"We must make a list of suspects," I say.

We tour the campsite, keeping our eyes open for anyone acting **suspiciously.**

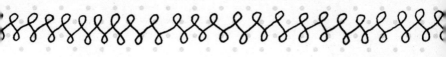

"What about those ladies who were having tea at the Nook yesterday?" I suggest. "There could be something fishy going on—**they actually COLLECT teapots!**"

We put them at the top of the list.

"And that grumpy old couple," says Beans. "Look—they have *flowers* on their windowsill. Maybe they wanted more!"

"And what about those little children from the **huge** tent?" I say. "I bet they could be quite naughty!"

We see Fred go past, pushing a wheelbarrow **full** of straw. "And Fred!" says Beans. "Who knows what's under all that straw? We should add him too. . . ."

I'm not really sure why Fred would want a teapot and a vase but I keep quiet. It's **important** to consider all possibilities.

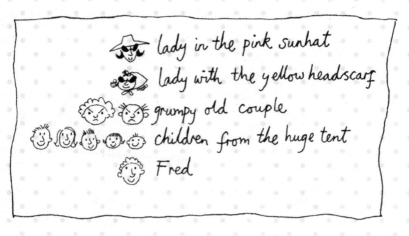

lady in the pink sunhat
lady with the yellow headscarf
grumpy old couple
children from the huge tent
Fred

But there's no time to discuss it further, because Mom is calling me over. She is making a **picnic lunch**.

"Grab your things," she says. "We are going to the beach!"

PATH TO THE BEACH

We meet up with Beans and his dad and follow the steep, stony path, winding down past **BLUNT'S BEACH CAFÉ**.

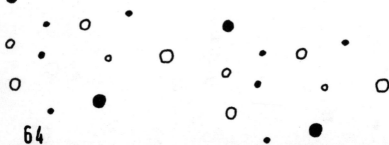

"Should we add Mr. Blunt to the suspects list?" I ask Beans. "He was at *the scene of the crime*."

"Yes, I think we should!" he says.

lady in the pink sunhat
lady with the yellow headscarf
grumpy old couple
children from the huge tent
Fred
Mr. Blunt

We turn the corner and there is a little cove and **THE SEA**.

We do not waste one single second—
me and Beans *rush* straight into the
waves, and so does McClusky!

EEK!!! It is MUCH **colder**
than I was expecting!

And it's MUCH harder to get out of a wet bathing suit than I expected too! Struggling to get changed inside a towel... *wiggling* and **wobbling** and *very* nearly falling over!

There is **sand** in the sandwiches but we don't care—the picnic is DELISH.

After lunch, we have a sandcastle competition—Beans and Maisy versus me and Alf.

The judges are my mom and Beans's dad. They say that both sandcastles are so *stupendously* good that we are **ALL** winners.

We stay at the beach **all day**. When
we get back to the campsite, there's
just time to change into our warm,
snuggly clothes before heading over
to Beans and his dad's tent for dinner.

It's a **BBQ**, followed by s'mores: marshmallows toasted on the campfire, sandwiched between two graham crackers with a layer of chocolate.

They taste INCREDIBLE.

While the grown-ups are chatting, Alf and Maisy are still whispering to each other, and McClusky is busy licking the **BBQ** dishes; me and Beans discuss the case.

"We will use our list of suspects and investigate each one—first thing in the morning!" I say.

"Great plan, Dot!" says Beans.

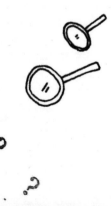

"We need to ask some cunningly clever questions," I say, "like, 'Do you drink a lot of tea?' and, 'Aren't the *flowers* nice at this time of year?'"

"And how about, 'Do you like **lighthouses**?'" adds Beans.

Beans also shows me a new way for us to send vital secret messages to each other across the campsite: MORSE CODE! He takes two small flashlights out of his pocket and gives one of them to me.

"You can send a secret message across a long distance. Each letter is made up of a different combination of a short burst of light—**a dot**—**and a long one**—a dash!"

"Dot dash—that's me in a *hurry!*" I laugh.

Here is the whole alphabet.

A • —	J • — — —	S • • •
B — • • •	K — • —	T —
C — • — •	L • — • •	U • • —
D — • •	M — —	V • • • —
E •	N — •	W • — —
F • • — •	O — — —	X — • • —
G — — •	P • — — •	Y — • — —
H • • • •	Q — — • —	Z — — • •
I • •	R • — •	

We try out our names.

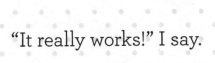

"It really works!" I say.

I use my new flashlight to look at the list of suspects again.

Hang on—what's this? Some of the note is missing!!!

Very strange...

lady in the pink sunhat
lady with the yellow headscarf
cross old couple
children from the huge tent
Fred
Mr. Blunt

Monday

Right after breakfast (Honey Nut Crispies from the campsite shop— YUM, my FAVE), Beans comes over.

SUNNY GLADES CAMPSITE

BEANS'S TENT

SHOP

SHOWERS & LAUNDRY

THE FARMHOUSE

BEACH

BIKE RENTAL

THE SEA

THE NOOK

PLAYGROUND

TEAPOT LADIES

MINI GOLF

BLUNTS BEACH CAFE

HUGE TENT

GRUMPY OLD COUPLE

DOT'S CAMPER

ANIMAL ENCLOSURE

WOODS

He has drawn **a map** of the campsite.

"Fantastic map, Beans!" I say.

THE SEARCH BEGINS. Me, Beans and McClusky head over to the bicycle-rental shed.

"We will cover much more ground on bikes!" I say.

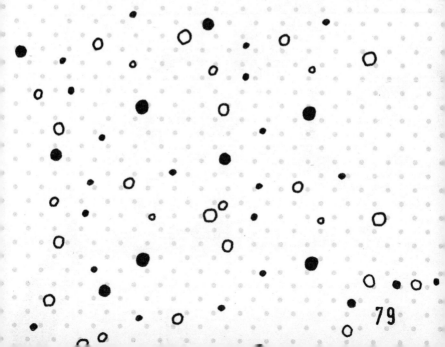

McClusky jumps up into my basket. He can be on lookout duty. He has a very good nose for **sniffing** out the **vital** clues.

First we cycle over to the camper van belonging to the ladies with the *pink* sunhat and the *yellow* headscarf. They are sitting at a picnic table reading their books.

Oh-so-casually, I say, "So, you collect teapots!"

"We *do!*" they say. "We've just bought these beauties at the local antiques market!" They proudly show us their rabbit teapot and their **cottage teapot** and another shaped like an airplane...

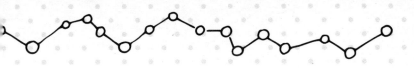

but no, **no**

lighthouse teapot

here.

~~lady in the pink sunhat~~

~~lady with the yellow headscarf~~

grumpy old couple

children from the huge tent

Fred

Mr. Blunt

Next we slow down near the little children's huge tent to get a good look at all the plates and mugs washed and laid out to dry . . .

but no lighthouse teapot and no vase of *flowers*.

"Do you like lighthouses?" Beans asks the children, but they just look at us, *puzzled.*

Then we prop our bikes up against a tree near the **grumpy** old couple's camper. Feeling very **nervous**, we **creep** around the side.

"You look first!" I whisper.

"No, YOU look first!" whispers Beans.

On tiptoe, we both pop up and **peep** inside.

Thank goodness there's no one there!
There ARE fresh *flowers*—but they
are in a different vase, not Poppy's.
No **lighthouse teapot** either.

~~lady in the pink sunhat~~
~~lady with the yellow headscarf~~
~~grumpy old couple~~
~~children from the huge tent~~
Fred
Mr. Blunt

We find Fred chasing an *escaped* chicken around the enclosure.

"Hot work!" says Beans. "Are you taking a tea break soon?" (So clever and *cunning*!)

"No tea for me!" says Fred. "Can't stand the stuff!" And he gets a bottle of cola out of his overalls.

"It can't be Fred then," I say. "Why would he want a teapot? And I don't think he's a vase sort of person either."

"We only have one suspect left on our list," says Beans. "Mr. Blunt!"

~~lady in the pink sunhat~~
~~lady with the yellow headscarf~~
~~grumpy old couple~~
~~children from the huge tent~~
Fred
Mr. Blunt

We return our bicycles and walk back.

At the Nook, we see Poppy balancing a **huge** pile of plates and teacups on one hand and putting up a notice for "Crafternoons" with the other.

Crafternoons!

Arty crafty fun at the Nook every Monday and Tuesday afternoon throughout the summer

come join us!

I am so excited! Poppy's Crafternoons are activities for the families staying at the campsite. Today's activity will be *decorating* cookies! **I REALLY** want to go and so do the twins.

Beans and his dad go out for the afternoon to see their Auntie Celia and Uncle Cecil who live nearby, so Mom takes McClusky for a walk and me and the twins go to the Crafternoon at the Nook.

"Why are you STILL wearing your big coats?" I ask the twins. "It's *so* hot today!" But they will **NOT** take them off. They are very *odd* sometimes!

Before we begin our *decorating*, Poppy brings out her special cookies and gives each of us one to try.

"I've never tasted this flavor before," I say. "It's SO YUMMY!"

"Ah, yes," says Poppy. "These are my grandma's SECRET recipe! Here, let me show you. . . ."

Poppy gets a book out of her apron pocket.

"It's my precious recipe book! This is where I keep all my very best recipes—I've been saving them for years. . . . I think that you are just the right person to appreciate it!"

We turn the pages together, looking at all her notes and pictures. Poppy loves to **doodle**—just like me!

The twins are on tiptoe to see too, but
I am *so glad* it was me Poppy chose
to show it to.

I LOVE

her recipe book—

it's amazing!

Poppy puts the recipe book down on
the counter, brings over more cookies
and a selection of *toppings*, and we get
started.

I am just concentrating on *decorating* my last cookie while the twins **scamper** around and won't sit still.

Poppy is `clearing` away the

sugar sprinkles

and **blobs** of icing, . . .

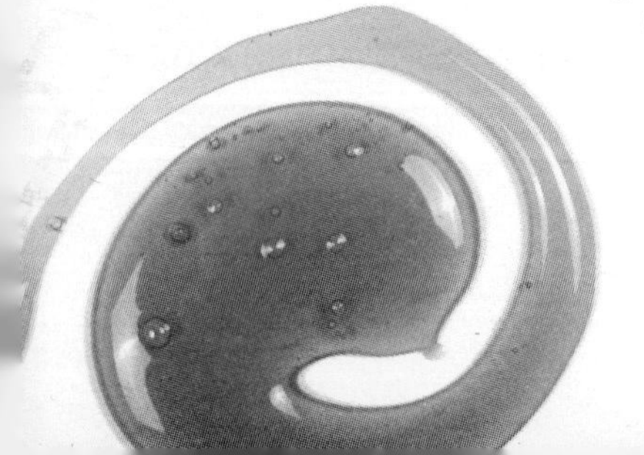

when she gives *a cry*.

The **sparkly** bunting has GONE!
Poppy feels inside her apron pocket . . .
looks at the empty counter . . .

HER RECIPE BOOK HAS GONE TOO!!!

OH NO! Another disaster!

"What **IS** going on?" says Poppy. I see she is nearly in tears.

"Don't worry," I tell her, "I'm sure they will turn up." I don't know what else to say.

Just as we are leaving,
I see Mr. Blunt again.

He is sneaking around the back of the
Nook and *peering* in through a small
window. Then he **stomps** away, back
down the path to his Beach Café.

HIGHLY

SUSPICIOUS.

Back at the camper, McClusky is playing with a massive stick he's brought back from his walk. I lie on the rug, munching my cookies, and do some crosswords in my **extra-big** new puzzle book, which always helps me

THINK.

First the **lighthouse teapot** and the vase
of *flowers*, now the **sparkly** bunting
and the recipe book . . .

And why is Mr. Blunt hanging around the Nook, **peering** in through the window?

Is he involved in the disappearances?

I'm **itching** to discuss it with Beans, but he won't be back until after dinner with his aunt and uncle.

Now it's bedtime. This is my chance to get a message to Beans!

"I'm just having one last look at the lovely MOON!" I say to Mom, and I step out into the **dark**. It feels exciting, being up and outdoors very late at night.

I get out my flashlight and send a 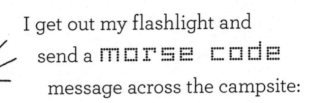 message across the campsite:

```
•• —• ••••— •   ••• — •• ——• •— — •
—— •—•
—••• •—•• ••—• ——• —
— ——— —— ——— •—• •—• ——— •—•
```

INVESTIGATE MR. BLUNT TOMORROW

I only hope Beans is looking.

He is! Here comes his reply. . . .

—·— · ···

YES

Just getting into my sleeping bag, and—strange! I didn't notice it before, but some of the note with the `morse code` alphabet Beans gave me is **missing....**

Almost as if it has been NIBBLED!!

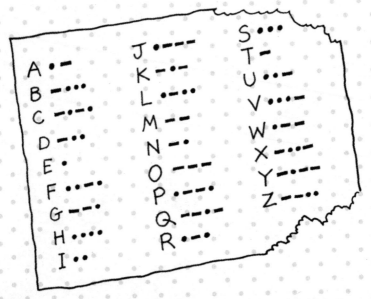

TUEsdAy

I don't even wait for breakfast—I grab an apple and **hurry** over to find Beans. But before we have even made a plan...

"LOOK—it's Mr. Blunt again!" I say. The chance to investigate him came sooner than we expected!

This time we **follow** him at a distance, making sure he doesn't **spot** us.

He **sneaks** up on the Nook when Poppy isn't looking . . .

First he **snoops** around the tables, examining the leftovers and *muttering* to himself, "Hmmm, very interesting...."

Then he pins up a leaflet advertising BLUNT'S BEACH CAFÉ *right on top of*

the Nook's sign—

WHAT A SNEAK!

And now he is hiding behind a tree, taking photographs of the Nook's menu board!

That settles it—Mr. Blunt is our number-one suspect!

"Mr. Blunt MUST be the thief!" I say.

"But **WHY**?" says Beans.

"Is he jealous of the Nook?" I ask.
"Does he want to make *his* café look
prettier and *his* cakes taste better?"

"And that way he hopes to **steal** the
Nook's customers!" adds Beans.

"We **MUST** get down to the
beach today to check him out!" I say.

"We can't let him see us **snooping** around and guess we're on to him, though," says Beans. "He's seen us a lot at the Nook already."

I frown. "But how will we get close enough to

BLUNT'S BEACH CAFÉ

without him

seeing

us?"

"I have a **brilliant** idea."
says Beans as his dad walks over.

! ! ! ! !

"Dad," he says, "can you lend us your
binoculars? We want to go
bird-watching!"

"Sure!" says his dad.

I rush back to our camper as fast as I can. "Please, please, *please* let's go to the beach RIGHT NOW!" I say to Mom. I am **SO IMPATIENT** to spy on Mr. Blunt and to solve this case!

Mom looks at me, surprised. "OK!" she says. **"Hold your horses!"**

At the beach, we use the **binoculars** to spy on Mr. Blunt from a distance.

We try and try, **peering** into the eyepiece and twiddling the focus, but it's still too **blurry** and **fuzzy** to see clearly into the café.

"Still **no** evidence!" I say. SO frustrating!

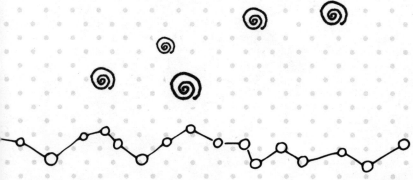

So we decide to leave it for now. We go snorkelling instead, then explore the rockpools with the twins. We see **a crab, a tiny fish,** and lots of **limpets**.

We always take buckets and **NEVER** a net. These **sea creatures** are really delicate— getting tangled in a net can hurt them!

After we let the sea creatures go, the twins fill their buckets with pebbles.

These buckets are *heavy*—I WISH I hadn't offered to carry them back up the path!

After lunch we have **three** rounds of mini golf . . . but I just can't get the ball in through the windmill door!

Today's Crafternoon activity is making a wind chime out of shells, bottle tops, and teaspoons.

Me and Beans go along, but we are too distracted discussing the case and our wind chimes end up a bit **wonky.**

ding!

ding!
ding!

In the evening, Beans's dad shows us how to make **monkey bread:** balls of cookie dough rolled in *cinnamon sugar* and baked on the campfire.

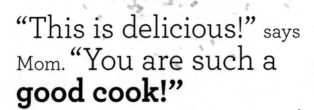

"This is delicious!" says Mom. "You are such a **good cook!**"

While the grown-ups are exchanging recipes, me and Beans plan the next stage of solving the **Sunny Glades** Mystery.

"We must get a closer look at **BLUNT'S BEACH CAFÉ**," I say. "There's nothing else to do. We need to go **DEEP INTO ENEMY TERRITORY...**"

? ? ? ?

WEDNESDAY

Beans and his dad come over for breakfast—**sausage sandwiches** with fried onions and ketchup.

On any other day I would LOVE them, but today I am too **nervous** to eat more than a few bites.

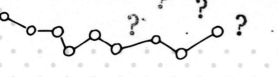

Right after breakfast, me and Beans persuade his dad to take us down to the beach.

On the way, we say hello to Poppy as she opens up the Nook. She is still *worrying* about the teapot and the vase and the bunting, but she misses her precious recipe book most of all.

"I just **can't** understand it!" she says.

"Don't worry—they will turn up **SOON!**" we say.

123

As Poppy brings out a tray of cake
and cookies, this gives me
an *idea.*

"We must try out lots of Mr. Blunt's baking,"
I whisper to Beans, "to see if he has been
using the recipes from Poppy's book!"

We don't bother with a swim or
sandcastles or anything else. . . .
Operation Enemy Territory starts

NOW!

While Beans's dad is reading the
newspaper, we walk right into Blunt's
Beach Café. My heart is beating
REALLY *fast* in my chest—

ba-doom-ba-doom-ba-doom!

We sit down at a table and look around. There is Mr. Blunt, serving behind the counter. In his hand—a teapot! Above his head—bunting!! On the table—a vase of *flowers*!!!

Have we caught *him* **red-handed**?

No.

It's not the lighthouse teapot—just an ordinary one. It's not the Nook's bunting either—not **sparkly**, just drab and **plain**. When we look again, we see the *flowers* are **plastic**, not even real.

"We still need to try LOTS of cake, though," whispers Beans. He is looking over at the cake stand and can't help licking his lips.

So we buy some cookies and a cupcake, and then **another** cupcake and some mini doughnuts, and then Beans buys **one more** cupcake "just to be sure . . ."

But they are *not NEARLY* as good as Poppy's. The cookies are just ordinary, nothing like Poppy's grandma's secret recipe.

Something catches my eye—
a poster on the wall advertising
**"Afternoon Activities
for all the Family"**
It reminds me of Poppy's
Crafternoons—the same but NOT
the same.

Is Mr. Blunt copying Poppy? Is that
why he has been *snooping* around
the Nook?

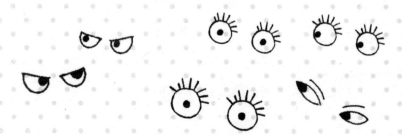

I have a

LIGHTBULB MOMENT.

"He's **stealing** the Nook's IDEAS!" I say.

"I think you're right! But we still have no proof," says Beans. "We must catch him in the act of **stealing ACTUAL THINGS!**"

This calls for

DRASTIC
action!

We make a SECRET plan....

It's evening and starting to **rain**.
Time to put on our disguises and
catch the thief **red-handed**!

 I have my *pineapple*
sunglasses and my hooded
beach cover-up with a
lobster pattern on it.

Beans wears a baseball cap

and a
stripy windbreaker worn like a cloak.

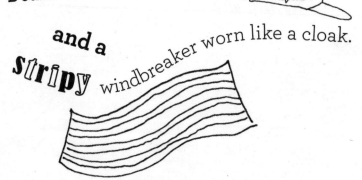

We dodge the showers, **sneak** around the back of the Nook, and hide behind a tree, peeping out. McClusky follows us—he always seems to know when he is needed. I'm glad he's here. He's not exactly fierce, but he is VERY protective.

Poppy has packed up all the **knickknacks** and is just about to close up for the day. While she is around the front, **stacking** the chairs, we **dash** into the tiny camper and quickly hide in the broom closet.

Beans finds a lampshade and pops it on his head—now we look even more like the pile of old stuff you might find in a closet. McClusky hides behind a **bristly** broom that looks very like him. He is a MASTER OF DISGUISE.

"Be VERY quiet, McClusky!" I whisper. "It's really important!"

"Im-PAW-tant?" says Beans.

"Don't make me laugh!" I whisper urgently.

When I get the **giggles** in a super-tense situation, it can lead to

HYSTERICS.

We wait and wait, **peeping** out of a tiny high window, wondering what Mr. Blunt might come to steal. Maybe Poppy's fossils, or her ornaments! Maybe her cups and saucers?

After a VERY

loooooong

time . . .

a *huge, scary shadow* goes past.

We are *terrified* out of our **wits!!!**
The shadow looms closer and an eye
peers in at us.

I am so *frightened* I cannot even
scream.

IS IT MR. BLUNT???

Massive

WHISKERY nostrils,
a rubbery pink tongue ...

NO—it is the donkey, *Please*. Or maybe it's Thankyou. It must have escaped from the enclosure, and is now wandering around the campsite—probably on the lookout for snacks.

I don't know whether I am more disappointed or relieved, but when we decide to call it a day and Beans hurries back to his tent and me and McClusky rush back to our camper,

my legs feel like wobbly jelly.

By now even the THOUGHT of Mr. Blunt scares me. I can hardly bring myself to look at my *doodle* of him, but when I do—half of it is **missing!** What **IS** going on? Is it sabotage??

Now there are TWO mysteries:

someone is stealing from the Nook, and something is happening to my **notes** and *doodles!*

Are these **two** mysteries connected?

It's night-time. I am woken up by the rain getting worse and worse, hammering on the roof, and the wind is **battering** against the windows.

There's a scritch-scratching noise *from under the camper.*

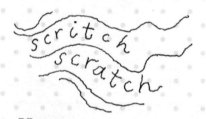

VERY creepy! I must be imagining it.

I put my head right inside my sleeping bag and try to get back to sleep.

Thursday

The rain has stopped, but because it rained so much in the night the grass has turned to **mud**. Alf and Maisy decide to roll down the **muddy** hill next to the play area.

They do it **again** and **again** and **again**....

The more **slippery** it gets, the *faster* they go and the better they like it. By now you can't even recognize them. They are two **mud-monsters** with feet.

And who joins in?
McClusky, of course!

Now the twins are making **mud** pies. *"Mmmm, yummy!"* they say. "It's our secret recipe!"

While Mom deals with McClusky and the **mud-monsters** in the shower, me and Beans have a hasty meeting of the Join the Dots Detectives.

Join the Dots Detectives HQ

We feel really down in the dumps. No evidence, no new clues. "What do we do now?" says Beans. But neither of us knows the answer.

Mom says, "You two look in the doldrums! How about some ice cream?"

After a cookies 'n' cream cone with sprinkles on top (me) and an *ice-cream sandwich* (Beans), we do feel a BIT better.

The twins turn down the chance of ice cream, preferring to play in the woods.

Strange!

Mom has given up trying to persuade them not to wear their big coats as they **march** back and forth.

We hang around at the campsite all morning, at loose ends. There's nothing worse than an **unsolved case**— but with **no new leads**, what can we do?

"Why not *play* with the twins?"

says Mom,
but they are busy emptying their
buckets and whispering in their *twinny*
language, so they don't need us.

"How about some bird-watching up on the cliff?" Beans's dad asks us, but we're not that interested.

"Take McClusky for a nice long walk," says Mom, and we do.

Me, Beans, and McClusky are just coming back past the Nook when we see Poppy at the hatch, looking very upset.

"A *fresh* batch of mini doughnuts— VANISHED!!" she says.

The doughnuts!!!

That's the **LAST STRAW.**
Poor Poppy.

The twins hurry over. "Come with us! Come with us!" they say.

But I'm hardly listening. "Not now," I tell them. This isn't the time for games—the case has taken an urgent new turn for the worse!

"Could it be one of the animals?" says Beans.

I think of the loose donkey yesterday and we rush to their enclosure. But there are *Please* and Thankyou, contentedly munching their hay . . .

We **run** over to the chicken coop,
but the gate is securely **locked. . . .**

Then we spot Speedy the tortoise's
balloon in the undergrowth. Could he
be making off with a doughnut??

We chase the balloon to catch up with him. He is **surprisingly fast**!

Me in front, then Poppy, then Beans, then McClusky ... The twins follow, **running** along behind us....

153

but no. All Speedy has in his mouth is a bit of **squashed** dandelion.

No sign of the mini doughnuts ANYWHERE.

The twins are *pulling* at our T-shirts. "Come with us!" says Alf.

"Not now," I say. "This *isn't* a good time!"

"PLEASE!" says Maisy.

And now I start to think....

Why have the twins been whispering *secretively* all week?

Why did they insist on wearing big coats in hot weather—could they have been hiding something underneath?

Why were they hanging around in the woods when they could have been having ice cream? And what were they emptying their buckets for?

"OK . . ." I tell them.

The twins lead us—me, Poppy, Beans, and McClusky—to the wooded glade next to the camper.

And here are the **lighthouse** teapot and the vase of *flowers*, and the **sparkly** bunting hanging up between the branches . . . and here are the precious recipe book and the mini doughnuts. . . .

Alf and Maisy have made their own café in a little clearing among the trees!

IT WAS THE TWINS ALL ALONG!!!

For a few moments, I am exasperated and very angry. "It's **wrong** to take things that aren't yours. . . ." I tell them.

But then I see their *happy*, proud faces, and how well they have improvised, with leaves for plates and cushions for seats. And then I see a handmade sign taped up on the trunk of a tree in their funny, childish writing:

Poppy's place

"You work so hard and you are SO BUSY!" Maisy says to Poppy.

"We wanted to make a special place just for YOU!" says Alf.

I am worried that Poppy will be angry ... but she just *laughs*!

"Thank you so much!" she says. "This looks **AMAZING!**"

And then she says, "Hang on a minute...."

She hurries over to the Nook and
puts up her own sign:

CLOSED
back later!

"It's about time I took an
afternoon off!"

We all sit together in Poppy's Place.
We admire the **sparkly** bunting
and the *flowers* and Poppy shows
us some more of her special recipe
book....

* * * * * * * *

We **enjoy** the mini doughnuts—
McClusky especially—and they are
STILL the best we've ever tasted,
even though the sugar coating *might*
have gotten a bit mixed up with sand
from the twins' bucket....

And we all have the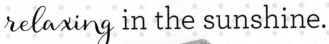
BEST TIME EVER,
relaxing in the sunshine.

Friday

The
last day of
Vacation!

But it's a lovely sunny day and there's still time for one last ice-cream cone and one more round of **mini golf**.

I knock the ball

right in **through**

the door of

the **windmill**.

YESSSSSSS!

And there's time for one last play on the beach. On the way down to the cove, we stop at a stream that goes alongside the path, right down to the sea. Perfect for a game of Poohsticks!

It's a race: we each choose a small stick, drop them into the water at the same time and see whose stick reaches the beach first.

We play again and again until everyone wins lots of races each.

So the **Sunny Glades** Mystery
is solved.

It was the twins who took the **missing things** from the Nook, but they did it for a kind reason. Mr. Blunt wasn't the thief after all, but he wasn't entirely innocent either. He *was* copying Poppy's ideas—that's why he was snooping around the Nook—and that is still a sort of stealing.

It didn't work, though—**BLUNT'S BEACH CAFÉ** isn't nearly as special as the Nook. It just goes to show you need to **think of your own ideas** if you want to be good at something!

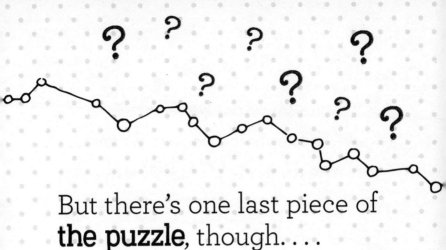

But there's one last piece of **the puzzle**, though....

Who has been **nibbling** my notebooks??

"Oh, that must have been Walter," says Poppy, "the resident campsite mouse!"

Sure enough, when we hitch up and move the camper, I see a little nest underneath made of **nibbled** pieces of paper from my notes!

So **THAT** was the
scritch-scratching noise
I heard on the night of the storm!

There's no sign of **Walter,** but when I look back at the picture of my *decorated cookies* from the Crafternoon, . . . there he is in the distance, hurrying off with a tiny scrap of paper. I hadn't spotted him!

We pack up the car and it is *even more* full of **stuff**—there's the twins' huge pebble collection, and McClusky insists on bringing his massive stick.

We say goodbye to Poppy.

"Come back SOON!" she says, giving us all a *big* hug.

There's just time for me to say to Beans, "That was our **trickiest** case of all—and the answer was right under our noses all along!"

"Yes!" says Beans. "See you back at home. There's lots of summer vacation left—**HOORAY!**"

goodbye! goodbye! goodbye!

Have you read?

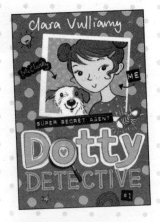

When someone seems set on sabotaging the school show, Dot is determined to find out how, and save the day!

When Dot starts hearing strange noises at night, Beans is convinced there has to be something SPOOKY afoot. But, before they can be certain, Dot and Beans must GET PROOF.

Dot and Beans can't wait for their exciting school trip to Adventure Camp! But why is someone trying to spoil the fun?

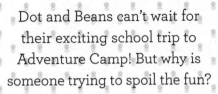

Dot's friend Joe has a cute new sausage dog puppy, Chorizo! But when she goes missing, the Join the Dots Detectives must track down the lost little dog. . . .

Dot and her teacher Mr. D. are both super excited about their birthdays. But then Mr. D.'s surprise present is stolen. Who could have taken it? It's up to the Join the Dots Detectives to find out!

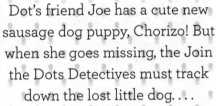

The end